I HERO

ATLANTIS QUEST
MENACE FROM THE DEEP

Steve Barlow and Steve Skidmore
Illustrated by Jack Lawrence

First published in 2014
by Franklin Watts

Text © Steve Barlow and Steve Skidmore 2014
Illustrations by Jack Lawrence © Franklin Watts 2014
Cover design by Jonathan Hair

Franklin Watts
338 Euston Road
London NW1 3BH

Franklin Watts Australia
Level 17/207 Kent Street
Sydney, NSW 2000

A CIP catalogue record for this book
is available from the British Library.

pb ISBN: 978 1 4451 2867 2
ebook ISBN: 978 1 4451 2868 9
Library ebook ISBN: 978 1 4451 2869 6

1 3 5 7 9 10 8 6 4 2

Printed in Great Britain by CPI Group (UK) Ltd

Franklin Watts is a division of Hachette Children's Books,
an Hachette UK company.
www.hachette.co.uk

How to be a hero

This book is not like others you may have read. You are the hero of this adventure. It is up to you to make decisions that will affect how the adventure unfolds.

Each section of this book is numbered. At the end of most sections, you will have to make a choice. The choice you make will take you to a different section of the book.

Some of your choices will help you to complete the quest successfully. But choose carefully, some of your decisions could be fatal!

If you fail, then start the adventure again and learn from your mistake.

If you choose correctly you will succeed in your quest.

Don't be a zero, be a hero!

You are a member of a Special Forces naval unit. You are an expert diver and can pilot submarines of all types. You are also a specialist in underwater combat, and have taken part in many dangerous missions. Your bravery and skill have won you many medals.

You are currently on a training exercise in the Pacific Ocean, teaching a group of recruits how to board a ship and rescue a crew taken hostage by pirates. You are directing the operation from a stealth boat, when you detect a fast attack craft closing in on your position. You scan the horizon and see it has no markings to identify it.

You immediately bring the weapons systems online and order the crew to action stations.

Go to section 1.

1

"Captain, our tigershark torpedoes are ready to fire," says one of your crew.

"Fire on my command," you reply.

The boat is less than half a mile away when a message blasts out over the comms speakers. "Code rainbow alert! Code rainbow alert!"

You have never heard of a "code rainbow alert" before. You wonder whether this is a trick to stop you attacking.

If you want to attack the boat, go to 47.

If you want to find out what "code rainbow" means, go to 26.

2

"I've planted mines on the hull of your ship. They are going to explode in five minutes," you boast.

"Thank you for telling me," replies Hydros. He barks out orders to his guards. Some hurry away, while others tap at control panels.

You wait while five minutes pass, and there is no explosion.

Hydros smiles at you. "It seems that my

divers have found the mines and deactivated them! I think your usefulness has ended."

He draws a harpoon gun, aims it at you. As you rise to your feet he pulls the trigger. You feel a surge of pain in your chest, then nothing more as you drop to the floor, dead.

You shouldn't have told Hydros about the mines! Go back to 1.

3

Half an hour later you and Shen are in the Barracuda, speeding under the waves towards the top-secret island base.

You are still curious about the Atlanteans living beneath the seabed. "Why aren't the Atlantean ships crushed by the pressure of the water at such a depth?" you ask.

"They have developed pressure shield generators that protect their ships," Shen replies. "Unfortunately, we don't have that technology on board the Barracuda."

"We could do with one if we're going to push them back into Atlantis. Maybe we should capture one of their ships and get hold of a

pressure shield generator."

"First, we have to stop them getting the missiles."

At that moment the Barracuda's computer voice fills the cabin. "Incoming SMART torpedoes. Thirty seconds to impact!"

To take evasive action, go to 45.

To launch the Barracuda's torpedoes, go to 24.

To ask Shen what to do, go to 17.

"We're here, so let's take out some of these bad boys!" you say.

You launch a volley of torpedoes, hitting several Atlantean fighters. But as the enemy ships begin to fire at you, you realise that you have made a mistake. You are badly outnumbered.

"Activate countermeasures," you order.

Explosions rock the Barracuda as more Atlantean ships join in the attack.

"There are too many torpedoes!" warns Shen.

There is a massive explosion which rocks the Barracuda. Water begins to flood the floor, just before the walls around you implode.

You have died. Go back to 1 to try again.

"We need to get to the island as quickly as possible," you tell Shen. "Jet boost it is!"

Shen switches the Barracuda's propulsion system to jet boost. You are thrown back into your seat as the submarine shoots through the water.

You are soon approaching the island. "Prepare to attack," you order.

Suddenly the Barracuda comes to a jarring halt. You look out of the cockpit window and see it is caught in a giant steel net. There are dozens of these traps! The Atlanteans were expecting you!

The 3-D image of an enemy sub appears on your control panel. "Enemy ahead," warns the Barracuda. "Nautilus Cruiser."

It is heading towards you, and you are trapped!

If you wish to try to blast your way out of the net, go to 28.

If you wish to try to use the Barracuda's engines to work your way free, go to 42.

6

Fifteen minutes later you are sitting in the submarine's operation room. The walls are lined with charts of the world's oceans displayed on huge 3-D screens. Admiral Crabbe sits at the table opposite you.

"So, what is ORCA?" you ask.

"ORCA deals with any threats to humankind that occur within the world's oceans, or in this case, from under the world's oceans."

You look puzzled. "You mean under the seabed?"

The admiral nods. "What do you know about Atlantis?" he asks.

You laugh. "Atlantis is a legendary city. The Greek writer Plato wrote about it nearly 2,500 years ago. It was a great empire, but it sank into the ocean. Some people think it really existed, but the reality is that Atlantis is just a story. I hope you're not wasting my time with this nonsense!"

Admiral Crabbe stares at you. "Let me tell you the real story of Atlantis."

If you want to listen to Crabbe, go to 15.

If you don't have time for stories and want to get on with the quest, go to 31.

7

You cut your sub-aqua bike's engine. The enemy divers surround you and point their dart guns. You raise your hands, but suddenly realise that the Atlanteans are a people who show no mercy.

Their captain gives a command and the water is filled with razor darts and, immediately afterwards, your blood.

You have paid the ultimate price. Go back to 1.

8

"Taking evasive action!" you say, moving the Barracuda. The super sub swings around, but gets caught in another steel trap! The Nautilus Cruiser closes in and fires its water cannon.

"Activate countermeasures!" you shout.

"They only work against torpedoes!" Shen screams.

You realise that you have made a fatal mistake.

The Barracuda has been destroyed, taking you and Shen to a watery grave. Go back to 1.

9

"Tell me more about the Atlanteans," you say. "And how do you know they are threatening the world with destruction?"

"We received this communication from their leader," replies Crabbe. The 3-D screens light up showing a video of four amphibious creatures. One of them begins to speak.

"People of the Land. I am Triton, king of the Atlanteans. For too long we have been kept captive in our kingdom under the sea. But now we are free. My warriors will wage war on you. Hydros will lead the way."

The screen goes blank.

"Who is this Hydros?" you ask.

"He is one of Triton's three commanders," says Shen. "The other two are called Hadal and Tempest — they are very dangerous."

"What else do I need to know?" you ask.

If you already know about the Barracuda, go to 29.

If you haven't found out about the Barracuda, go to 22.

10

"Is there another way to destroy that thing?" you ask Shen.

She thinks. "We could attach urchin mines to the hull, close to the engine room. If enough were detonated together it would blow open a hole. Then we could programme the Barracuda to launch torpedoes into the engines, and its power source. That would do it!"

"How do we get close enough to the ship to attach the mines?" you ask.

"Use a sub-aqua bike," replies Shen. "It's small enough not to be detected by their scanners. The problem is it would take longer than a frontal attack. But it gives us a better chance of destroying the ship."

To attack the mother ship head on with the Barracuda, go to 36.

To use the sub-aqua bike, go to 23.

11

"Activate pressure cannon. Engage and fire."

A stream of superheated high-pressure water heads towards the Ray Fighter. It smashes into the vessel, but does little damage.

"We're too far away for the cannon to work," Shen realises.

The Ray Fighter turns towards you and opens fire with a barrage of torpedoes. Shen activates the countermeasures, protecting the Barracuda from a direct hit. "Quickly! Fire torpedoes!" Shen shouts.

Go to 33.

12

You send a message to the incoming boat: "Identify yourself immediately."

After a few tense seconds a voice comes over the speakers. "This is an ORCA vessel. Admiral Sanchez has given us permission to talk to you about a top-secret...quest."

You smile. Sanchez is your boss. "Permission to come aboard," you reply. You wonder what the quest could be.

Minutes later the attack craft pulls up and two uniformed agents step onto your boat.

You introduce yourself. "So what is ORCA?" you ask.

"The Ocean Research Central Agency," the female agent answers.

You shake your head. "I've never heard of it."

"You're not supposed to," snaps the man. "It is an ultra top-secret agency. We have a situation and need your expertise."

You don't like the man's attitude. "Well, you learn something every day. But I'm busy. I'm running a training mission. Pirates are big trouble these days."

The man snorts with derision. "Pirates? The quest we have is bigger than any pirates. The future of humanity is at stake. We need you to come with us. Now."

If you want to complete the training mission, go to 19.

If you wish to take up the "quest", go to 38.

13

When you wake you find yourself on the floor of a command centre. Standing over you is a figure you recognise – he was standing in the background of the video you saw. It is Hydros!

He smiles. "Welcome to my ship."

"Why haven't you killed me?" you ask.

"I have decided to spare you for the moment so you can see the capture of the missiles from the island. I will take them back to Triton and your puny ships will not be able to follow us."

You remember about the pressure shield generators that the Atlanteans possess.

"I also wish to know what you were doing outside my ship."

You realise that the Atlanteans haven't found the mines! You glance at your watch — you have been unconscious for twenty-five minutes and there are only five minutes before the mines detonate. You will be trapped in the ship when they explode!

If you want to tell Hydros about the mines, go to 2.

If you don't, go to 44.

14

You have no time to rest as the Barracuda once again warns you. "Enemy ship one kilometre ahead. Atlantean Ray Fighter."

"It's a single-seat fighter," says Shen. "That's

what fired the torpedoes at us. It must be on a scouting mission."

If you wish to attack it, go to 40.
If you wish to let it go, go to 49.

15

"OK, I'm listening," you reply.

"Three thousand years ago, Atlantis really did exist," begins Admiral Crabbe. "But it wasn't human beings who lived there. It was inhabited by a race of amphibians. They are called Atlanteans. Their sea-based technology is more advanced than our own."

You shake your head. "You said 'are called', like these Atlanteans still exist."

"They do," replies Crabbe.

You laugh. "Amphibians? Like mermaids and mermen?"

"No, the Mer people are different."

"Oh, come on," you say. "Mer people! You're kidding me."

Crabbe presses a button. "Send in Shen."

The door opens. You gasp in astonishment as a tall female figure steps in. She has gills and a

fin runs down her back.

"This is Shen. She is a Mer. They are the people of the deep..."

"Pleased to meet you," says Shen. "Don't be so surprised, and do close your mouth — you'll catch a fish!"

"Shen is going to be helping you with the quest."

Go to 43.

You decide that more mines are needed and continue to attach them to the hull.

You manage to place two more before you swim towards the Atlantean divers. You don't want them to see the mines.

They begin to shoot at you. You spin the bike around and manage to dodge their razor

darts. You return fire and take out a couple of the enemy, but you realise that you are outnumbered.

If you wish to surrender, go to 7.
If you wish to fight on, go to 34.

17

"What's the best option?" you ask Shen.

"Use countermeasures. They are ultra-fast little rockets that target enemy torpedoes."

"OK, do it."

The countermeasures shoot away and hit the torpedoes just in time. The explosions rock the Barracuda, but cause no damage.

Go to 14.

18

"Let's get to the base," you tell Shen. "We need to stop the attack."

You switch the Barracuda to stealth mode and head towards the island.

As you get closer to your destination, you see dozens of motorised tanks scuttling along the seabed, heading towards the island.

"Crab tanks," says Shen.

"Where are they coming from?" you ask.

"There must be an Atlantean mother ship nearby," replies Shen. "It will be the command centre for the attack."

"I bet that's where Hydros will be," you say. "But Admiral Crabbe's orders are to get to the island and keep the Atlanteans occupied until reinforcements get there."

To search for the mother ship, go to 32.
To head to the island, go to 41.

19

You shake your head. "I've never heard of ORCA and I've got a job to do here. I think I'll decline your offer of saving humankind."

The man stares at you. "I told my boss that you weren't up to it." He turns to the woman. "Let's go."

They return to their boat, leaving you wondering what the quest could have been.

When you feel up to undertaking the quest, go to 1.

20

"We'll use stealth mode," you tell Shen. "I don't want the Atlanteans to track us."

"But Admiral Crabbe said use jet boost," she replies.

"He's not here," you say and switch on stealth mode.

An hour later you are still making your way

to the island when Crabbe's face appears on the video comms screen. He looks furious.

"Where are you?" he shouts. "The Atlanteans have taken over the base and captured the missiles! Earth is at their mercy!"

You've made a big mistake. Learn from it and go to 1.

21

You wait for the explosion...

5... 4... 3... 2... 1...

You clench your fists.

There is a muffled blast and the mother ship shakes. Lights flash and a few alarms sound, but then these stop.

Hydros barks out orders to his guards, who check the control systems and report back.

"It seems that your explosives did not breach the hull," Hydros says. "You have failed and failure must be punished!"

He draws a harpoon gun, aims it at you and pulls the trigger. You crumple to the floor, dead.

You didn't pack enough punch! If you wish to begin again, go to 1.

22

"We need to show you something," says Crabbe. "Come with us."

You follow Shen and the admiral through the vast corridors of the submarine. Finally, you arrive at a large steel door.

Crabbe taps at the keypad and the door opens. In a dock in front of you is a streamlined submarine. You've never seen anything like it before.

"This is the Barracuda," replies Crabbe. "The Mer people helped us to build it. It is the most advanced sub in the world. Shen will tell you all about it."

Shen shows you around the Barracuda.

"It is amazing," you say. "But why are you showing me this?"

"We need you to pilot it," replies Crabbe.

If you already know about Triton, go to 29.
If the admiral hasn't told you about the Atlantean threat, go to 9.

23

"I'll use the sub-aqua bike," you say. "You load the mines and program the bike autopilot, so I can attach them in exactly the right place."

You put on an aquasuit, while Shen carries out your orders.

"I've set the mines to explode thirty minutes after setting them," Shen explains. "That should give you enough time to get back to the Barracuda."

"I'd better be quick then," you smile.

"You can attach the mines using the robotic

arm or swim out and attach them," Shen tells you. "There's a chance that the ship's scanners will detect the bike so near to the hull, but it will take longer if you swim."

You nod. "I'll decide when I get to the ship. You stay here and keep the Barracuda hidden until I return."

Soon you are heading towards the mother ship on the sub-aqua bike. The autopilot takes you to the spot where the mines must be attached.

You radio back to Shen. "In position. Ready to deploy mines."

If you wish to use the robotic arm to attach the mines, go to 48.

If you wish to swim over to attach them yourself, go to 30.

24

"Launching torpedoes," you say.

"That's not going to work," cries Shen. "They're SMART torpedoes..."

You see what she means. The incoming torpedoes simply dodge your torpedoes and head towards you.

Shen shrieks, "Activating countermeasures!"

But it's too late. There is a huge explosion and a flash of light as the Barracuda is blown apart.

You have failed! To begin again, go to 1.

25

"We need to know more about the ship," you say. "Run a scan."

Shen obeys. Within seconds a 3-D hologram of the ship is displayed on the control screens. You scan through the data file.

"What's the probability of a successful frontal attack?"

Shen shakes her head. "Practically zero..."

To attack the ship anyway, go to 36.

If you want to find another way to destroy it, go to 10.

26

You check for a "code rainbow" on your computer. A data file comes up.

"Code rainbow refers to all ORCA vessels."

You are still puzzled. You type "What is ORCA?" The screen goes blank.

The fast attack craft is getting nearer. You have to make a quick decision.

If you wish to attack, go to 47.

If you wish to make contact with the approaching boat, go to 12.

27

"I'll deal with the divers," you tell Shen. You turn the sub-aqua bike around and head for the incoming divers.

You open fire with the sub-aqua bike's sea dart missiles. The explosions take out a couple of the enemy. They return fire but you easily dodge their razor darts as you spin the bike through the water. Again you fire at the Atlanteans, and again your aim is good. Another enemy falls to your attack.

However, the other fighters split into two sections to outflank you. You can't fight both groups. You are in big trouble!

If you wish to surrender, go to 7.

If you wish to fight on, go to 34.

28

"Fire water cannon!" you order.

A stream of high-pressure water hits the steel nets and rips them apart, releasing the Barracuda.

But you are not out of danger just yet. "Nautilus Cruiser closing in," Shen warns. "We should get out of here."

To attack the enemy sub, go to 37.
To take evasive action, go to 8.

29

Admiral Crabbe scowls. "Our sonar scouts and unmanned underwater vehicles have detected a large fleet of underwater craft heading towards a volcanic island in the Pacific."

"So?"

"The island is home to a top-secret missile base. We think that the Atlanteans want the brand-new rocket technology that is being developed there."

"Then send over some cruisers and blast them out of the water," you suggest.

"We already have," says Crabbe. "The

Atlanteans have wiped out every vessel that was sent to intercept them. The only ship that can get there in time and take on the Atlanteans is the Barracuda. You have to get to the island and stop the Atlanteans getting the missiles. And that's just the first part of the quest. If you do that, then the next step is to drive the Atlanteans back under the seabed."

"It's a do-or-die mission," says Shen.

"Then what are we waiting for?" you say.

Go to 3.

30

"I'm going to attach the mines myself," you radio Shen.

You stop the bike, pick up a mine and swim to the mother ship.

Shen's voice comes over your headset. "You've been spotted! The scanners have picked up a squad of enemy divers heading your way!"

"I've only attached one mine!" you say. "How long before they reach me?"

"A couple of minutes," replies Shen.

"I won't be able to swim to the bike and get

back in time to attach more mines," you say.
You get back to the sub-aqua bike just as the divers arrive.

Go to 27.

31

You shake your head. "I'd rather find out about the quest."

Admiral Crabbe bangs his hand on the table. "You have a serious attitude problem! Atlantis is the quest. And you need to know about it. Are you ready to listen?"

You nod meekly.

You swallow your pride. Go to 15.

32

"Maybe we should look for the mother ship. If we destroy it we'll stop the attack," you say.

Shen nods. "I'll scan for it."

Soon you are heading away from the Atlantean fighters and searching for the mother ship. Within minutes Shen finds it. "Enemy fifteen hundred metres, bearing 310 degrees."

"Bring up visual." You gasp. The ship is huge!

"Leviathan class," the Barracuda tells you. "Command mother ship."

To attack the ship, go to 36.
To find out more about it, go to 25.

33

"Torpedoes locked on! Fire!"

The torpedoes speed through the water and hit the Ray Fighter. The Atlantean vessel disappears in a massive explosion.

You report back to Admiral Crabbe, who tells you that the missile base is already under attack from the Atlantean fleet. The troops there are holding out, but time is running short.

"Get to the island and try to keep the Atlanteans occupied while we get reinforcements to the base. Use jet boost to get there." He signs off.

Shen looks concerned.

"What's the problem?" you ask.

"If we use jet boost, we won't be able to use stealth mode," she replies. "The Atlanteans will know we are coming. But if we don't use jet boost, we might get there too late."

If you wish to use jet boost, go to 5.

If you decide to use the stealth mode, go to 20.

34

You decide to carry on fighting and draw the divers away from the mines.

Razor darts from their weapons fizz through the water, but you manage to avoid them.

However, there are too many enemy fighters

for you to keep track of. A explosion behind you sends shock waves through the water. You are thrown off your bike and pass into unconsciousness.

Go to 13.

35

The screens fill with a picture of a great doorway in the seabed.

"This entrance to New Atlantis is 15,000

metres under the sea," explains Crabbe. "It is at such a depth that no submarine can reach it — it would be crushed. That's why Shen's people guard the entrance."

"Just a minute," you say. "The Mariana Trench is supposed to be the deepest point of the seas, and that's only 10,900 metres deep."

"That's what we want people to think. We don't want people to panic." Crabbe looks grim. "The Atlanteans have broken through the seabed. Shen's people are desperately trying to find out where exactly. In the meantime, the Atlanteans have threatened humans with total destruction. And that's why you are needed."

If you want to know more about the Atlanteans, go to 9.

If you want to know about your quest, go to 22.

36

"We should attack now," you decide.

Shen protests, but you ignore her. You steer the Barracuda towards the mother ship and launch a barrage of torpedoes.

As you do so, the vessel's huge metal doors open. Dozens of Atlantean Ray Fighters pour out. Hundreds of torpedoes head your way. Your mouth hangs open.

"Deploy countermeasures!" Shen orders, knocking you to one side. "We need to take evasive action," you cry, but it is hopeless. There are too many enemy vessels. A torpedo hits, taking out the Barracuda's power systems.

The Atlanteans move in for the kill, and in a flash your world implodes.

Go back to 1.

37

"We could get trapped in the nets again," you say. "We're going to attack! Lock on torpedoes and fire."

The Barracuda's torpedoes launch. The Nautilus Cruiser takes evasive action and avoids one torpedo. The other one strikes, forcing the ship into one of the Atlanteans' own steel nets. The Nautilus is trapped! It tries to break free, but cannot. It is helpless.

If you wish to destroy the cruiser, go to 46.

If you wish to leave it and get to the island, go to 18.

38

"Saving humanity? Sounds interesting," you reply. "How do I sign up?"

"You come with us," the man replies.

You hand over the training mission to your second-in-command, and follow the ORCA agents to their boat.

Soon you are heading out into the ocean. After an hour of travelling, the boat comes to a stop in the middle of nowhere.

At that moment the boat begins to rock violently as a submarine emerges from the water. It looks nothing like any sub you have ever seen.

"Welcome to ORCA's HQ," says the woman. "Admiral Crabbe is waiting for you."

Go to 6.

39

You wait for the mines to detonate...

5... 4... 3... 2... 1...

There is a series of explosions and the mother ship rocks. Huge explosions follow as the Barracuda's torpedoes strike the engines and the Leviathan's power source.

Lights flash and alarms sound. Walls begin to buckle and seawater starts to pour in. The Atlanteans rush around in total panic.

Hydros snarls at you, points his harpoon gun and fires. You just manage to dodge the deadly missile. He aims his weapon at you again. "This time I will not miss," he snarls.

At that moment, there is another explosion and the command centre's window shatters. As

water floods the room, you are astonished to see Shen appear on a sub-aqua bike! She opens fire at Hydros, hitting him before he can shoot you. The Atlantean commander floats away in a cloud of inky blue blood. Shen passes you a

breathing apparatus. You quickly put it on and grab onto the bike.

As you head to the safety of the Barracuda, you glance back to see the Atlanteans abandoning the mother ship. The Atlantean ships that were attacking the island are fleeing by diving back down into the depths.

Go to 50.

40

"We can't let it report back," you say.

Shen agrees.

"So it's time to see what the Barracuda's weapons can do!"

If you wish to attack with torpedoes, go to 33.

To attack with the pressure cannon, go to 11.

41

"OK," you say. "We'll get to the island and see what we can do to stop the attack."

As you approach the island, the Barracuda's 3-D scanner is full of moving dots, showing at least thirty Atlantean vessels attacking the island with rockets and sea-to-surface missiles.

"Are you sure we're doing the right thing?" asks Shen.

If you wish to attack the Atlantean ships, go to 4.

If you wish to try to find the mother ship, go to 32.

42

"Reverse engines, full power," you order. The Barracuda strains against the steel net, but cannot break free.

"Enemy attack imminent," warns the Barracuda.

"Forward, full power," you order. Again the submarine thrusts against the net, but remains trapped.

Shen shouts, "Do something!"

But it's too late. The Nautilus cruiser fires its water cannon and you disappear in a fiery explosion.

The Barracuda has been destroyed, taking you and Shen to a watery grave. Go back to 1.

"Tell me what this quest is," you say.

"Reveal the Atlantis quest," Crabbe says.

The 3-D screens light up, showing images of strange sea creatures. "The Atlanteans weren't happy being just rulers of the sea," says

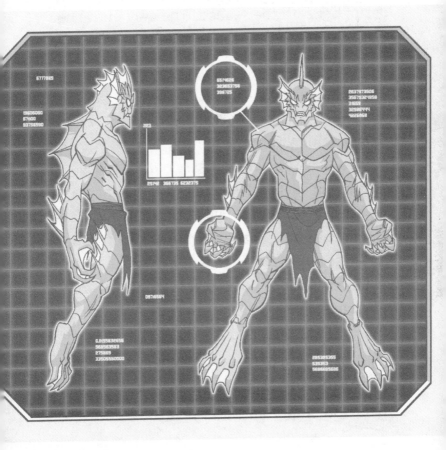

Crabbe. "They wanted to take over the land and waged war against humankind. But we had an ally — the Mer."

Shen continues the story. "The Atlanteans enslaved my people. We rebelled against them and, after a long war, together we finally defeated them. They were exiled to an ocean realm beneath the seabed. The only entrance was sealed and guarded by my people."

Go to 35.

44

By not telling Hydros about the mines, you realise that you will probably die, but you shake your head. "I was just trying to find a way in," you reply as you struggle to your feet.

"You did that," laughs Hydros.

You look at your watch. There is one minute until detonation! You brace yourself for what is to come.

If you fixed one or two mines to the hull, go to 21.

If you attached four mines to the hull, go to 39.

45

You swing the Barracuda away from the incoming torpedoes, but they change course and continue to head towards you.

"Fifteen seconds to impact," warns the Barracuda's computer voice.

"We won't be able to shake these off," says Shen. "They are SMART torpedoes — intelligent and deadly!"

"Can't we use our torpedoes?" you ask.

"No, they'll just avoid them."

If you want to launch the Barracuda's torpedoes anyway, go to 24.

If you decide to ask for Shen's advice, go to 17.

46

"Moving in to destroy the enemy," you say.

The Barracuda moves slowly towards the trapped Atlantean ship.

At that moment a huge claw swings round from the Nautilus and grabs the Barracuda.

"Warning. Hull at critical pressure," the Barracuda's computer voice says.

But there is no escape. The Barracuda is crushed between the giant pincer.

You are fish food! Go back to 1.

47

You decide to attack. "Fire torpedoes," you order.

The tigershark torpedoes launch. The incoming ship stands no chance. The torpedoes hit and the boat erupts in a massive fireball.

"Target destroyed," confirms your crew man.

Minutes later a message comes in over your satellite phone. It is Admiral Sanchez, your boss. "You idiot!" he shouts. "You've just destroyed an ORCA vessel. It was coming to collect you for a top-secret quest. Didn't you receive the code rainbow alert?"

You don't know what to say.

"Get yourself back to base," continues the admiral. "You'll be answering to a military court for what you've done." The line goes dead.

You shouldn't have attacked! There's no place on a quest for hotheads like you. Cool down and return to section 1.

48

You decide to attach the mines as quickly as possible and use the robotic arm. You begin to load up the mines into the robotic arm and then move the bike into position. You attach the first two mines to the hull without any problems.

Shen's voice comes over your headset. "You've been spotted! The scanners have picked up a squad of enemy divers heading your way!"

"I've still got more mines to attach," you say. "How long before they reach me?"

"A couple of minutes," replies Shen.

"I won't be able to attach all the mines," you say. You wonder if two mines will be enough to blow open the hull...

If you want to attack the divers, go to 27.
If you want to continue to attach the mines, go to 16.

49

"Let's wait and see what it does," you say.

Shen disagrees. "It's attacked us. It knows

we are here. It's probably reported our position already. We have to attack."

"No. We can follow it to find out what the Atlanteans are up to," you say.

A few minutes later, the scanner's screen fills with dozens of white dots moving at incredible speed.

"Enemy ships closing in," warns Shen.

The screen shows hundreds of torpedoes heading towards you.

"Evasive action! Deploy countermeasures!" you cry, but it is too late. There is a flash of light and the Barracuda is ripped apart.

To start again, go to 1.

50

The next day, you and Shen are back on board ORCA's HQ with Admiral Crabbe.

"You both did a great job," says the admiral. "Destroying the mother ship stopped the attack on the island. The Atlanteans didn't get hold of the missiles. The ships that got away have headed back into the depths."

"Shame we can't follow them," you say.

The admiral smiles. "But we can. We've managed to salvage the pressure shield generator from the Leviathan mother ship — we can fit this to the Barracuda. It means the super sub will be able to dive to unlimited depths. Now we can take the fight to the Atlanteans and force them back under the seabed. We still have more work to do, though. I'm sure that Triton is not going to be happy about losing one of his commanders, and he's going to be cooking up new plans!"

The admiral looks grimly at you. "It's going to be a tough mission. We don't know what dangers you'll face. Are you still up for the quest?"

You nod. "Of course I am..."

You are a hero! Thanks to you the Earth and humankind is safe...for now...

TOP SECRET: ORCA Barracuda

(1) Stunfish launcher –
self-propelled weapons
resembling sunfish that
produce a low-frequency
sonic wave to knock
out enemy defences.

(2) Crew cockpit –
where the Barracuda
pilots sit.

(3) Countermeasures –
ultra-fast mini-rockets that
target and destroy enemy
torpedoes.

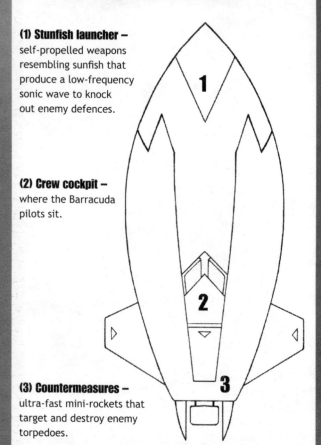

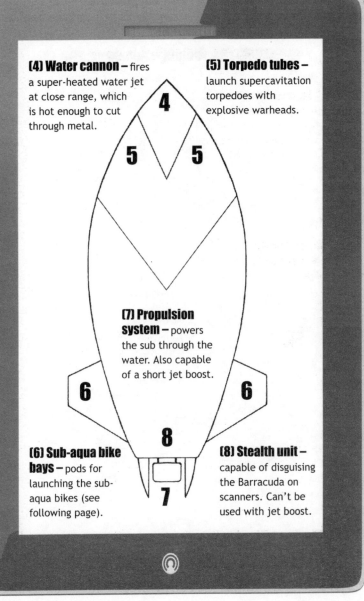

(4) Water cannon – fires a super-heated water jet at close range, which is hot enough to cut through metal.

(5) Torpedo tubes – launch supercavitation torpedoes with explosive warheads.

(7) Propulsion system – powers the sub through the water. Also capable of a short jet boost.

(6) Sub-aqua bike bays – pods for launching the sub-aqua bikes (see following page).

(8) Stealth unit – capable of disguising the Barracuda on scanners. Can't be used with jet boost.

TOP SECRET: Barracuda – sub-aqua bike

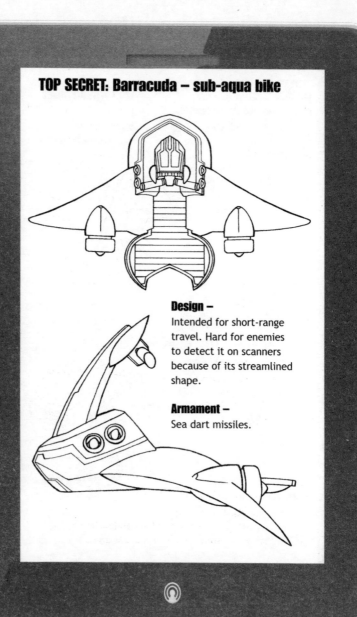

Design –
Intended for short-range travel. Hard for enemies to detect it on scanners because of its streamlined shape.

Armament –
Sea dart missiles.

TOP SECRET: ORCA weapons technology

Urchin mine –
High-explosive charge that can be fixed to a target and set to detonate by timer or motion sensor.

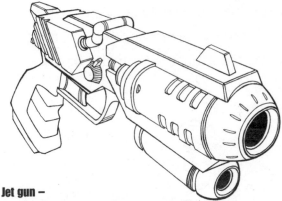

Jet gun –
Short-range weapon that is capable of firing barbed projectiles underwater. Also has a launcher that can fire flares, and self-propelled stun and high explosive grenades.

You and Shen are taking the Barracuda for a test dive to see how well the captured pressure shield generator works. You have already reached a depth of 10,000 metres.

"To get to this depth without any problems is extraordinary," you say. "This shield is incredible."

Shen nods. "We will need it if we are going to find the hole in the seabed where the Atlanteans broke out."

Before you can reply, an alarm begins to wail. "Warning! Crush depth exceeded! Outside pressure too great," warns the Barracuda...

Continue the adventure in:

ATLANTIS QUEST 2

OCEAN ALLIANCE

I HERO
DECIDE YOUR OWN DESTINY
EDGE
ATLANTIS QUEST
OCEAN ALLIANCE
Steve Barlow - Steve Skidmore

About the 2Steves

"The 2Steves" are
Britain's most popular
writing double act
for young people,
specialising in comedy
and adventure. They

perform regularly in schools and libraries,
and at festivals, taking the power of words
and story to audiences of all ages.

Together they have written many books,
including the *Crime Team* and *iHorror* series.

About the illustrator: Jack Lawrence

Jack Lawrence is a successful freelance
comics illustrator, working on titles such as
A.T.O.M., Cartoon Network, *Doctor Who
Adventures*, *2000 AD*, *Gogos Mega Metropolis*
and *Spider-Man Tower of Power*. He also works
as a freelance toy designer.

Jack lives in Maidstone in Kent with
his partner and two cats.

Have you completed the other I HERO Quests?

Battle with aliens in Tyranno Quest:

AIR BLAST
Steve Barlow - Steve Skidmore
978 1 4451 0875 9 pb
978 1 4451 1345 6 ebook

FIRE STORM
Steve Barlow - Steve Skidmore
978 1 4451 0876 6 pb
978 1 4451 1346 3 ebook

ICE STRIKE
Steve Barlow - Steve Skidmore
978 1 4451 0877 3 pb
978 1 4451 1347 0 ebook

EARTH ATTACK
Steve Barlow - Steve Skidmore
978 1 4451 0878 0 pb
978 1 4451 1348 7 ebook

Defeat the Red Queen in Blood Crown Quest:

SANDS OF BLOOD
Steve Barlow - Steve Skidmore
978 1 4451 1499 6 pb
978 1 4451 1503 0 ebook

DRAGON MOUNTAIN
Steve Barlow - Steve Skidmore
978 1 4451 1500 9 pb
978 1 4451 1504 7 ebook

DEMON SEA
Steve Barlow - Steve Skidmore
978 1 4451 1501 6 pb
978 1 4451 1505 4 ebook

CITY OF THE DEAD
Steve Barlow - Steve Skidmore
978 1 4451 1502 3 pb
978 1 4451 1506 1 ebook

Also by the 2Steves...

978 0 7496 9283 4 pb
978 1 4451 0843 8 eBook

A millionaire is found at his luxury island home – dead! But no one can work out how he died. You must get to Skull Island and solve the mystery before his killer escapes.

978 0 7496 9284 1 pb
978 1 4451 0844 5 eBook

The daughter of a Hong Kong businessman has been kidnapped. You must find her, but who took her and why? You must crack the case, before it's too late!

978 0 7496 9286 5 pb
978 1 4451 0845 2 eBook

You must solve the clues to stop a terrorist attack in London. But who is planning the attack, and when will it take place? It's a race against time!

978 0 7496 9285 8 pb
978 1 4451 0846 9 eBook

An armoured convoy has been attacked in Moscow and hundreds of gold bars stolen. But who was behind the raid, and where is the gold? Get the clues – get the gold.